A Springtide Meeting

EMILY MURDOCH

ISBN: 1983802026
ISBN-13: 978-1983802027

DEDICATION

To my readers. Thank you for your loyalty.

And Joshua.

CONTENTS

ACKNOWLEDGMENTS

A huge thank you has to go to my incredible family – and those friends who have become family.

Thank you.

CHAPTER ONE

Thursday 4th March, 1790. London
Dear Dr Walsingham,
Well, you have succeeded. I am coming to Weymouth, and it is all your fault of course. Sea air? Rest? I do not consider myself in any way elderly at this point, and yet familial pressures and your conniving now mean that I am to make the long journey from London to Weymouth, jolted all the way no doubt on a second-class carriage with a second-class driver. I hope you are happy with yourself, Dr Walsingham, for I certainly am not. You can alleviate your conscience, however, by meeting me on the Wednesday after I arrive at your doctor's surgery, where you can identify me by my large golden heart-shaped locket, undoubtedly obvious in the sunlight, and give me a full — and clean — bill of health.
Until we meet, and most probably after that, I shall remain,
Miss C Honeyfield

Monday 5th March, 1790. Weymouth
Dear Miss Honeyfield,
Since our correspondence began, your brother (an acquaintance of my cousin, as you know), has been most desirous that your health be considered seriously. I am delighted to hear that you will be joining me in Weymouth; its health benefits alone are reason enough to visit, but

beyond that there is thriving society that I am sure you will enjoy. I am quite at your leisure, yet sadly my surgery itself has been closed for some months for refurbishment. I will, however, happily meet you on the promenade opposite the Esplanade – shall we say, eleven o'clock? The springtime March air may be chilly, so wrap up warm. The last thing that I would want, as your doctor, is for you to catch cold whilst waiting for me.

I am your ever-faithful servant,
Dr Walsingham

The golden sand rippled in the wind, and scattered over her skirts. Toes bare, she lowered them and Cordelia could not help but smile with delight as the grains of sand pushed against her heel. She had left her stockings behind, a risqué move but one that was surely more common here? A salty breeze tugged at the curls that had slipped from her pins, and her smooth skin pulled at the gloves keeping the breeze from her.

She had done it. She had made it to Weymouth.

"Weymouth," Cordelia Honeyfield murmured under her breath, her thirsty eyes absorbing everything that was going on around her. Elegant couples dressed in the latest French fashions, bonnets rustling in the wind, were strolling arm in arm up and down the promenade. She was sitting on the edge of the walkway, legs dangling down to the sand, and gulls with dark heads were bobbing along the lapping tide.

Admittedly, Cordelia had not done it alone.

"Wrap that shawl a little closer around your shoulders, Cordelia," came the sharp tones of Mrs Chambers. "And mind you keep it there, this wind is biting. And where are your gloves?"

Cordelia had not noticed. She had almost forgot that Mrs Chambers, the indomitable chaperone, was standing behind her under a parasol almost stolen by the wind, and she had almost forgot about the odious Dr Walsingham. The disgust rose strongly here, but receded as she watched another small fishing boat pulling onto the shore.

"Look, Mrs Chambers, another one!" She flung out a finger as she spoke excitedly, but there was no answer from her companion, who shook her head at her young impetuous charge.

Three men jumped out of the small boat, and began to haul it further up the sands, sweat pouring from their brows despite the spring breeze that bit at uncovered flesh.

I could go anywhere, she thought. This is not London, or home – there is nowhere in Weymouth that I cannot go, any time that I wish. The mere possibility of such freedom was enough to get her pulse racing, and colour in her cheeks.

". . . perhaps today."

She caught the dribs and drabs of conversations that passed her along the promenade.

"Today? Surely the King is in London, he would not bring his family down here so soon –"

"Nay, I swear it, that is what I read, and he is going to bring his . . ."

The pair of ladies, past the prime of life and greying at the edges, moved beyond Cordelia's ears, but as her gaze followed them it rested on a gentleman.

He was not moving along the promenade; he was standing, perhaps ten feet from her, staring out to the ocean. Dressed in all the finery that one would expect from a gentleman, he was not doing anything as far as she could tell. Just standing there.

Cordelia turned back to watch the fishermen complete their journey, but they had already taken their spoils further inland, and now that she was aware of the young man out of the corner of her eye, she found that she was uncomfortably conscious of him. Was he watching her? If she turned her head to see, was she watching him?

A flush that had nothing to do with the liberty before her started to creep up her neck. This was as bad as waiting around for the last half an hour for Dr

Walsingham – was he ever to arrive? Thinking of him again made her irritation with him rise like bile, and she quashed it.

"Mrs Chambers, I wonder if –" Cordelia began, turning around to speak to her chaperone; but she had gone. The only person standing behind her now was the young man, and his eyes, previously vague in their focus, had found something to lock onto. Her.

He should not be staring at her – certainly not now that she had noticed, though his expression was surely blatant enough for her to feel discomfort. But Dr Timothy Walsingham could not help it. A young lady, seated alone at Weymouth was enough to draw the eye regardless of her personal charm, and this woman had more than enough.

Perhaps it was her chestnut hair that drew the eye; the way that the struggling springtime sunshine glinted off it, as it did the waves from the sea. Perhaps it was her figure, slender and small. Perhaps it was the way that her shoes lay carelessly forgotten beside her. But more than anything else, it was probably the way that her eyes seemed to have flecks of gold in them as the sun sparkled in them. He had only seen them for an instant before she turned to gaze back out to sea, but they seemed to be constantly altering their colour, at once a light brown and at others a hazel. Had he imagined flecks of shimmering gold?

And to top all that, Timothy could see that she had followed the latest fashions in beachwear, and underneath the woollen shawl wrapped tightly around her neck and shoulders, was wearing a dress that was several inches shorter than the urban style, displaying pale ankles and half of her calves to the world as they swung down to the sand.

This is ridiculous, he chided himself. You are a doctor, not some young whelp of a boy coming up to Oxford! Should a few inches of bare flesh really turn you into such a – an animal?

The answer, unbidden and mercifully unspoken, came back to him immediately: yes. This was not a young woman that you came across often.

But this was not the time to stare down unaccompanied young women who could have come to Weymouth for the delights of the coming season. He was here to find the elderly lady whom he had been advising by letter, and poor old Miss Honeyfield seemed, if the letters be true, in dire need of a little medical attention. He had waited here at least thirty minutes, but none of the more mature ladies who had strolled up or down the promenade before him had been wearing a golden heart-shaped locket matching the one she had described in her last letter.

Something golden did catch his eye though, and he was drawn as though by a magnet back to the young woman, her back resolutely turned to him. The sea air, gusty as it was this spring, lifted a curl of hair and the lock glinted golden in the sunlight.

Timothy realised that his mouth was open.

"Catching flies?"

At first, he did not understand who had spoken, but by process of elimination if it had not been he to speak first, then it must have been –

The woman's eyes, no longer fixed out to sea, were staring at him filled with suspicion. Timothy closed his mouth slowly.

"Because I would have thought you would have more success with honey, if I were you."

Timothy willed himself to speak, but for some reason, no sound came out. His lips did not even move. He was too busy drinking in that sharp look of interest he could see in her face.

She furrowed her brows as she beheld him. Then she turned around to watch the waves, now stronger as the tide turned.

"I was watching the ocean." Relieved that he could speak again, Timothy took a step forward towards the young woman, gaze fixed upon her, and almost barrelled into a mother with a child either side of her. Muttered apologies were offered before he found himself on the other side of the promenade, standing beside the seated young woman.

"I love watching the tide," was the reply from her, and Timothy smiled. "I have always loved the sea, rarely as we have visited it."

"You have been here before then?"

She nodded slowly, not taking her eyes from the cresting waves that shone first blue, then silvery white. "When I was a girl, and before the Royal family had ever thought to come here – it was not a fashionable place to come to, then."

It did not take long for Timothy to make a decision. Leaning down, he dropped to sit beside the young woman, leaving a respectable two feet between them as decorum would dictate. From here, he could see much more of her, and was surprised to see that there was a hint of sadness playing around her mouth, despite the smile.

"Some people just love the sea," he said quietly.

She turned towards him, and the smile deepened to something more genuine. "It is as though salt runs through my veins, rather than blood."

Timothy nodded. "That is an admirable way of putting it; many people seem to come alive when they arrive here. Something in the air, something in the water sparks them into life like nothing else."

A gull, squawking into the gusty breeze, floated by them. The control was absolute, only needing to move its wings minutely to guide itself along the beach, calling out to its friends.

"It is funny though," she said softly. "I seem to spend the majority of my time considering the ocean, and I have not yet set foot in it. I have a friend from home who has gone swimming in it! But that is a pastime far beyond me – I do not even know how to swim."

He smiled. He caught a fleck of golden light dancing in her eyes as she spoke. "It is recommended here, of course, for its health benefits, but I must admit that there are plenty of us who live here in the town who swim for the pleasure of it."

At his words, she turned to stare at him. "Swim – for pleasure?"

Intensity sparked through her, and Timothy's smile broadened. This strange woman seemed to give her companions all her attention, or none of it. "Yes, for the sheer joy of it. There is nothing quite like being out in the water, completely lost in the elements. If you are not careful, you can forget that there is even a real world around you."

She stared at him, and then smiled slowly. "To be perfectly honest with you, I shall be sad to leave here after a fortnight."

An overwhelming feeling of disappointment washed over him. "Is your stay so short?"

"Short?" The young woman stared, puzzled. "How do you know that I only arrived but recently? I could have been here five weeks already."

"Oh, I live here," said Timothy quickly, "and I observe whenever there is a new person in Weymouth, and therefore I assumed that –"

"I have to go." Before he could say anything more to reassure her that he had not, in fact, been following her as she undoubtedly seemed to think, she had pulled herself up and placed her sturdy shoes on her feet. "I must meet Mrs Chambers – goodness knows where she has got to, she was supposed to be my chaperone."

No one had intrigued Timothy more than this woman, almost a mermaid in her devotion to the sea, and she was already stepping away from him. He did not even know her name.

"Miss – excuse me, Miss?" He scrambled to his feet, and waved an arm after her, knowing better than to follow her.

The breeze caught his words and flung them out to sea, far away from her ears. She had not heard him, and he was already losing sight of her in the crowded street that led on from the promenade.

Timothy sighed. Sometimes it was just not meant to be.

". . . and why you considered it acceptable to simply leave me there, alone, I have no idea." Cordelia had rattled off her speech and did not even pause to hear Mrs Chambers' reply. Stalking upstairs, she went to her room, and sat, irritably fiddling with the quill on the wooden desk that had been provided for her.

Cordelia reached out for a sheet of paper, and there was a roughness to it; there were grains of sand under her fingertips as she brushed past it. She could not help but smile. There was sand in her shoes also, and every step reminded her that she was here, finally, in Weymouth. Now all she had to do was get this meeting with the odious Dr Walsingham over, and she would be free to do what she wanted here – father or no father.

The quill was dipped into the inkpot, and after dabbing it slightly to rid it of its excess, she began to write.

Wednesday 10th March, 1790. Weymouth
Dr Walsingham,
It is with the greatest of regret that I remind you that you did not fulfil our appointment this afternoon; honestly, it is too bad of you, when I have come all this way from London and you cannot even stir from your fireside chair. No matter, Dr W, I am sure that I will not hold it against you forever – and fortunately for you, there is an opportunity most providential to atone for your crime. I shall be in the same place tomorrow morning – that is Thursday morning, Dr W, so as to prevent you from wilfully misunderstanding – at eleven o'clock. Same place, same time, different people. After all, you did

not bother to attend.

Do not disappoint me again, sir. There is much that I wish to do here, and I cannot spend the week waiting around for you. I am ever your patient patient,

Miss C Honeyfield

CHAPTER TWO

Dr Timothy Walsingham tugged at his greatcoat, and pulled it closer around him as the biting spring wind attempted to wrench it open. A squall was coming in, and the whole of Weymouth could feel the icy wind. His top hat, usually proud upon his head, was grasped underneath his arm for fear of it being blown off. Turning a corner – and knowing that as it brought him to the beach, the wind would only increase – he braced himself.

And almost gasped audibly.

There she was. A day later, and there was the same young woman, this time standing, at the same place on the promenade.

Legs almost entangled themselves as Timothy tried to stop himself from going forward, desperate not to be seen by her, but it was too late. Her face had twitched up, and a look of surprise mingled with alarm covered it – an expression that was probably mirrored, he thought ruefully, on his own.

Why was she here again? It was too much to hope, and he smiled briefly, that she was here in the expectation of seeing him again. Their conversation the day before had been brief; it surely could not have sparked in her an interest.

But why not? It had done, within him.

Unsure what he was supposed to do with his hands and feeling an almost uncontrollable urge to whistle, Timothy stood still, allowing the gusting wind to buffet him slightly forwards and backwards as the cry of the seagulls made for a mournful melody.

As the seconds turned to minutes, Timothy gazed around him. The unsettled weather had driven many of Weymouth's inhabitants and visitors inside, away from the gusting wind, and it could surely come as no surprise to him that Miss Honeyfield, the poor old dear, was staying safe inside. She had remarked in one of her letters, and he smiled to think of it, how clumsy she was, constantly tripping over her own feet and having to pass it off as the untidiness of the cobbles. No, Miss Honeyfield would not be venturing out today.

But she had. Another glance over at the elegant young woman, staring resolutely anywhere but where he stood, was enough to drive his impetuous nature.

"Good morning."

His words were snatched away by the breeze but, unlike the day before, they were pushed towards her rather than away from her. She nodded, and Timothy took a step closer.

"I hope you are well, this fine morning, and not concerned about the wind." The weather. He was talking about the weather? Cringing inside, he glanced over to her to see if his ineptitude and forwardness had made her wish to leave.

It seemed not.

"I love the wind, do not you?" Cordelia stretched out her arms and glorified in the way that the wind caught at her shawl, wrapped tightly around her neck and shoulders. "Does it not make you feel as though you could take off at any moment, and join the birds in the air?"

Closing her eyes, she turned, revelling in the sharp

scent of the salty wind that rushed through her hair.

"It is certainly a day to feel alive." The young gentleman who had appeared again seemed slightly concerned about her sanity, and Cordelia put down her arms and opened her eyes. The last thing she needed was word to get back to her father that she was unstable.

Cordelia smiled serenely. "Indeed, sir. There is nowhere one can feel alive quite like Weymouth."

The man took another step closer to her and rather than take a step backwards herself, as she would have done in London when a man she did not know got too close, she stayed. Their brief meeting the day before somehow settled her spirits. There was something about this man that made her feel entirely safe; as though he were some sort of anchor, unmoveable and unshakeable despite the tugging of the world.

And his next words shocked her.

"I was wondering if you would enjoy taking a stroll down the promenade with me." His words were quiet yet firm, and as far as Cordelia could tell, there was no mischief in them.

She turned around. Mrs Chambers had only run back to collect her own shawl from their lodgings, and she would surely panic if she returned to this spot to find Cordelia absent from it. And yet the promenade was not so very long, and she was desperate for a walk. All this lounging around for one's health, there was nothing more likely to kill one off.

Cordelia decided. "I would be delighted, Mr . . ."

If she was not mistaken, there seemed to be a slight hesitation before he answered her, "Timothy. Just Timothy."

It was enough to make her pause. Surely it was his real name – surely, she could trust him, a gentleman as he was, dressed in that frockcoat with top leather boots, a large gold pocket watch chain slightly visible when the wind moved it. And after all, this was Weymouth out of season.

She would not want her full name to be known here either, to be written in the gossip pages of London as a feeble woman who could not stand life's challenges to the extent that one needed time away at a healing spa.

"And I am Cordelia." Her words were short and clipped, but there was no distrust in her tones. *I wanted to escape my father's control, after all,* she thought, *and here I am! He would never have countenanced such behaviour, but there are none here to stop me!*

Turning on her heels, she began to walk slowly along the promenade, the golden sand on her left and the jutting spit before her. Timothy, or whatever his name was, did not have to move fast to catch up however. It took him but three long strides to be alongside her. Cordelia looked over at him, and he smiled.

"Why have you come to visit Weymouth, if I may ask?"

Cordelia stopped to pick up a bit of dry seaweed, and glanced out to sea. "You may ask," was her short reply.

He seemed to accept this. Cordelia raised an eyebrow; a man who did not question, who did not demand to know everything, who was happy to accept an obvious rebuttal without censure?

It was this, perhaps, that made her relent. "It was my Papa."

Timothy smiled, and nodded reassuringly as the wind tried to steal the shawl from her shoulders. She pulled it tighter as he said, "He wanted you to enjoy the sea air, and have a holiday?"

"Ha!" Her sarcastic laugh was not lost on him.

"Perhaps not."

"Perhaps not indeed." Cordelia tore the seaweed that was in her hands to shreds, and smiled, amused, into her companion's face. "Nay, I should not laugh, not when such a holy man is involved. My brother has been newly ordained, you see, and the family is concerned about my health."

"Your health?" His eyes widened, and without thinking

13

he put out an arm to take hers – one that she escaped, and so his arm dropped to his side again. "Did you see many doctors in London?"

"Four . . . five? They all seem rather alike after a while, their grey beards waggling as they talk about 'spirits' and 'grave concern' and 'in need of a restorative trip'. If you ask me, it is because the style of corsets is too tight."

Her voice was light, but there was a sense of sadness underneath it. Timothy swallowed. "I did not realise that you were in need of Weymouth's restorative powers."

"Oh, I think that if Papa had been truly concerned about my health, I would have been sent to Bath, do you not agree?" A wry smile appeared on her face, and she shook her head as they passed a family with five children, the parents attempting to herd their children like lambs across the beach as one flock.

There was a second of silence, and Cordelia let it linger. It was rather exotic, not being known intimately by someone. Her entire acquaintance at home had known her for – goodness, twenty years or more! How delicious to be able to pick and choose the information that one reveals, to only have known about oneself what one decides to impart – to live as a mystery if she wanted to!

But this Timothy was not an aficionado of mysteries. "What symptoms were you experiencing, that a trip to Weymouth was necessary?"

Cordelia could not help but laugh at this, her fingers grasping another stray strand of seaweed from the bank beside them as the spit came closer into view. She could feel the cold movement of her locket underneath her shawl as she walked. "Timothy, I know we have only just met, but you will soon learn to see through my idiocy and dissembling. Fear not, I am not about to keel over before you; I am here not for a sea cure for fainting fits, but for exuberance and over-excited spirits."

With these words, she skipped ahead of him, turning around and walking backwards to face him. "In truth," she said beaming, "I am here to cure my one true fault: that I always want my own way, in everything."

Timothy could not help but burst into laughter, alarming the two young ladies that passed them. "Cordelia, you are incorrigible!"

She batted her eyelashes, and almost tumbled over as her foot caught on a pebble. "Why, thank you for saying so, kind sir!"

"Your father cannot manage you, and you have been sent here as a sort of . . . punishment?"

His voice sounded surprised and a little censorious, and Cordelia examined him. He could not be much older than she, and he had money, otherwise the top hat would have stayed at home. Who would risk losing it, if it could not be replaced? He seemed in the habit of charming, that was for sure, and yet he seemed genuinely unsure how to manage her.

She sighed. Add him to the list, then.

"Not a punishment, really," was her eventual reply. "Dearest Papa conspired with a doctor to have him recommend a sea visit."

"Conspired!" Now it was his turn to laugh. "I was not aware that doctors conspired with anyone."

Cordelia's smile became more mischievous, but there seemed to Timothy to be sadness mingled in with it. "And yet here I am."

She twisted back to face the spit, and Timothy was left with the view of her back – a sight still lovely, it had to be said. And so, this was why Cordelia was here: a doctor who believed that the sea air would calm her spirits.

"I have met such doctors, of course, and disagreed with them." Timothy had wondered who had spoken – and then realised that it had been himself. His train of thought, so personal, had escaped him and entered the world. At what price?

Cordelia had turned to stare at him. "You have?"

He nodded. "I do not think that women should be

punished for feeling alive, as men are allowed to do. What does that gain, but servile partners to our lives?"

And then he almost walked into her, stopping himself short as she had done mere moments before a collision. Her eyes were wide, her mouth open, and the seaweed that had been in her hand had dropped to the ground, forgotten.

"Do you genuinely think that?" Cordelia asked quietly, hands clasped around her shawl, keeping it tight around her. "Truly?"

A gust of wind pushed her, and she raised a hand to his chest to prevent her from falling. They stayed there.

"Truly," he murmured. His arms had moved, almost without his knowledge, and cradled her elbows to steady her, but it was now that he felt the movement of her ribcage as she breathed. Her lashes fluttered as their eyes met, and he could see her breathing quicken.

What are you doing man, it has been moments since you met the woman – unchaperoned, and unprotected!

The idea burned through his mind and he dropped her arms and took a step backwards as though she was red hot.

"And . . . and you decided to come after all?" He managed, walking around her and continuing towards the spit. "You do not strike me as a person who would allow such a thing to happen if you did not secretly wish it."

He did not turn his head, but could feel her presence by his side, and then heard her speak.

"I must admit, the doctor in the letters does seem to be genuinely concerned about my health," Cordelia admitted in a low tone. "It is hard to truly dislike someone who is so amiable. And besides, if I had my way, I would always live by the sea," she confessed, fiddling with what he could see was another piece of seaweed, dried out in the sun. "Being within earshot of the waves, tasting the salt on the breeze – it is more than I can bear lodging at the Golden Lion which to my mind, is far too much a distance from the shore."

"I must say, I think I undervalue the place that I live because I see it often." Timothy said, quietly. "You see something every day and then you start to go blind to its charms."

But who could ever go blind to her charms? He wondered. This woman was part woman, part mermaid, always slipping from his understanding.

"Cordelia," he began, not entirely sure where this sentence was going to lead him, "I was wondering if –"

"What is the time?"

She stared at him inquisitively, and Timothy thrust his hand into his waistcoat pocket to retrieve his pocket watch, hands resolutely clasped at the top of the face.

"It does appear to be midday," he said, almost disappointed. Whatever the reason she had asked, it was surely not one that kept her here, and his enjoyment of her company seemed about to be drawn to a close.

And he was right. "I must go. Mrs Chambers – that is my chaperone, you know, though you would hardly know it, consider us now! She is expecting me, if I had not met the dreaded doctor – thank you for the walk, sir."

Skirts flying in the wind and her haste, the woman he had met the day before sprinted down the promenade running faster than anyone Timothy had ever seen. In a flurry of shawl almost escaping and her muffled laughter, she was gone.

That evening, two letters found themselves switching residences.

Thursday 11th March, 1790. Weymouth
Dr Walsingham,
Well, what is this – another disappointment, and it is all your fault so do not think about crying to me. I waited for you at least ten minutes, which is more than anyone should be required to do in polite society, and I eventually gave you up as a lost cause. I have come here on your instructions, if you remember, and the least you could do is

face me after you have brought me here for my health. It should not take long; all I require of you is to see that I am perfectly well, and that is an end to it. I am sure you have plenty of women on your books who cannot spare you for even a minute – but they must, as I am your most irritable patient,

Miss C Honeyfield

Thursday 11th March, 1790. Weymouth
Miss Honeyfield,

I am beyond desperately sorry to have missed you today. Indeed, my other patients are being just as neglected, but I am to make amends within the day, and I shall attend to you first – shall we say, nine o'clock? I would be remiss, however, if I did not ask where you were this morning when I waited for you – but no matter, I am sure you had a most elegant and correct reason for leaving me waiting. If you would wear that golden heart-shaped locket that I have heard so much about, I am sure it will not be difficult to give you a quick medical examination, and then a clean bill of health. I remain, most affectionately, your devoted,

Dr Walsingham

CHAPTER THREE

Cordelia burst out laughing. "You, again?"

Friday seemed to be handing her the same view that Wednesday and Thursday had offered; a tall man in a rather large greatcoat, though no top hat under one arm, despite being less windy than the day before. He turned, and a rather surprised smile spread over his face.

"Why – Cordelia, I had not expected to see you here again!"

There was something strange about the way that his words spread over her like a warm sunrise, but she put it down to a lessening of the wind. It could not be, of course, his Grecian profile or the way that he seemed pleased to see her.

"Nor I you," she returned, walking towards him and taking in a lungful of fresh salty air. "Your acquaintance has not arrived, then? I say acquaintance because I think if you had been waiting for a friend, you would have had much less patience."

Timothy's eyebrows rose. "Less patience? You do not think, then, that for our friends we should have almost unlimited patience, as those who love us dearly?"

He inclined his head at an elderly gentleman who

passed them along the promenade, so Cordelia was not sure whether he had caught her snort of laughter – it was suppressed as she wrapped her shawl around her tightly against the biting wind, her fingers grazing past the locket from her mother that she always wore, and when his gaze returned to her, her features were elegantly composed.

"For our friends, we typically have but little patience, for they know us well and should be ready to accept and forego any shortcomings." She spoke decidedly, striding forwards towards the edge of the promenade and taking both shoes off. "They can easily offend and easily be forgiven – but an acquaintance, someone who does not know our faults? For them is our patience, surely. After all, they have not had time to learn of all our faults yet."

The laugh Timothy gave seemed borne more of confusion than mirth, but Cordelia could not tell exactly; her eyes were focused on the rolling waves, and her mind on the sensation of the sand between her toes. In truth, there was nothing to compare to it.

"Perhaps you are right," came Timothy's voice ever closer, and Cordelia felt rather than saw him drop beside her. "And you are right about my acquaintance; she is an elderly gentlewoman, a friend of the family whom I have never met. All I know of her visit here is that she is staying at the Golden Lion, and –"

"The Golden Lion?" She physically started, a jolt that knocked her into him. "But that is where I am staying, Mrs Chambers and me. What a coincidence!"

"It is indeed strange, considering just how many different lodging houses, inns, and hotels there are now in Weymouth," Timothy conceded. "And yet five years ago, in 1785, it was rare for there to be any sort of number of visitors, making extra accommodation not necessary. Have you seen her?"

Cordelia dragged her gaze away from the ocean, confused. "Her?"

He stifled a laugh. He had never met anyone so easily

distracted by the constantly changing scenery of the seaside. Woe betide the elderly Miss Honeyfield to come across this vibrant and vivacious Cordelia. "My correspondent. I know little of her, but I think she must be of advanced years. She writes sometimes as though she has lived over seventy years on this dull plain."

"My word, she sounds formidable," smiled Cordelia. "I shall certainly keep a weather eye out for her."

Sighing, he shook his head. "I fear that she is too ill to leave her rooms as she has come to Weymouth —"

"For her health?" She should not have allowed the bitterness to creep into her voice, but she could not help herself. "Poor thing, she has probably been bundled off by a family member — younger, and poorer, no doubt — in the hope that she will catch a sea chill and die off, leaving her fortune to the next generation!"

Timothy laughed, and clasped his hands together in his lap. "That is as may be, but I can assure you that I would profit none by her death — so you can assure yourself that I am no murderer!"

She smiled back in turn, and cast a glance over to him past dark lashes. "I did not have you down as a murderer, sir, I have more than enough of those from the circulating library's novels!"

At this, he sat up straighter. "Ah, you have found the one here — here in Weymouth? It is perhaps my favourite place, other than the shore itself, in the whole town. Have you been there recently? There is a new book by William Gifford that I have been most desirous of reading myself, but I have not yet had the opportunity to attend."

"No time like the present!"

Without another word, she had jumped up and taken a few steps away from him, until his words caused her to stop.

"Cordelia, will you not be needing these?"

She turned to see her shoes being held at the end of his fingertips, a knowing smile on his face. She could not help but smile.

"Perhaps," she conceded. "I rather enjoy walking barefoot, I must own, but it is one of those practices that my dear Papa is attempting to sand out of me, like a piece of wood with splinters."

Though one hand kept tightly on her shawl, the other reached forward and took the shoes from his, delicate fingers brushing past each other. The gasp that Cordelia let out was audible, and it was matched by him. It was as though a spark had jumped between them, something greater than themselves and yet emanating from them.

She dropped her gaze, and concentrated on putting her shoes back on her feet, pulling her ankles back towards her hips, and when she caught Timothy's eye, again, the moment had passed.

"Do . . . do you know the way to the circulating library?" He said, more to cover the silence than anything else. He drew himself up to stand tall as she replied.

"You know, I do not think that I have come across the one in Weymouth yet," she mused, looking left and right. "Which way?"

"'Tis not far." Timothy raised a hand, and she moved into him, staring out where his fingers pointed. "Just further along the shoreline. It is nearby York Buildings – you know, on Charlotte Row? Five steps from it and you are back on the sand again."

"Very well." She began walking, but Timothy did not join her side at first. Cordelia was surprised at the sadness that washed over her when he was not beside her – and the shiver of pleasure she felt when he was.

"You make your mind decisively," he said.

It did not seem to be a negative tone, and she nodded. "When you have spent most of your life in London, following other people's wills and instructions, being able to make your own becomes almost a joy in itself."

As they walked, they passed several couples arm in arm. Heat rose in her as she caught glimpses of his hand beside her, fingertips out of reach. He had not offered her his arm, and despite her inclination to take it, she restrained herself. This was not her brother.

The circulating library was situated in a tall terraced building, and Cordelia stood still before it, not moving.

Timothy had walked forward, but now paused. "Are you not coming in?"

"Not yet." Cordelia stared at the building, and the faint paint marks that denoted its contents. "I have got to drink it all in first. How many hundreds of books, how many thousands of pages, how many millions of stories are carefully bound in leather and placed on shelves in this place?"

He was staring at her, and a flush of self-consciousness rose in her. This was unusual; normally the outraged or concerned stares of other people lapped at her feet, not reaching her heart at all. This man was different.

There was sand in the entranceway, and sand throughout the rooms that had been ground into the carpets. When the wind blew northwards from the ocean to the shore, you could still smell brine on the air, and there was crystallised salt at the window panes.

"Good morning," piped up the gentleman who was tending the library. His black frockcoat was formal, and had golden buttons all the way down the sleeves. "Is there anything in particular that I can discover for you, sir, madam?"

Cordelia smiled. "There most certainly is, but first I need to adventure though the woodlands of your library. I shall be back soon."

She strode off into the depths of the shelves, and she could hear the answering beat of Timothy's footsteps behind her.

"I thought we were here for William Gifford?"

He had spoken in a whisper and she answered in one – though perhaps not how he had expected. "Do you not find it singular that people lower their voices when they enter a library? Almost as though they were churches, holy sites of treasures waiting to be discovered."

As soon as the words were out of her mouth, she regretted them. Was she never to learn the talent of holding her tongue? She may not agree with her father about her general 'ill health', but that did not mean that she should not learn an element of decorum.

"I think of them more as treasure islands."

Cordelia stopped dead in her tracks, and turned to stare at Timothy. He smiled.

"It strikes me as more accurate," he continued in a whisper, "that authors bury treasure in books, ready for us to stumble across when desperate for safe shores, and the more we read, the richer we become."

Her mouth opened, but no sound came out.

"Do . . . do you not think so?" He sounded hesitant, and she could not help but warm to him. How many other men gave their opinion so decidedly, but were perfectly happy to be challenged?

Her eyes glittered as she replied, "It is a beautiful notion, and one that I think we should take ourselves. Tell me, do you have a pocket book on your person?"

If he was surprised by her question, he did not show it. As they resumed their slow pacing up the corridor that the shelves had created, he handed over a small black leather-bound pocket book, along with a pencil.

"Thank you." Cordelia reached out for them both, and almost gasped audibly as his fingertips brushed over her palm as he placed them within it. Was this the heat of the day, or a reaction to that barest of touches? She shook her head slightly, as though trying to dislodge water from her ears, and then stopped before a large atlas that had been placed on a table, for the reference of patrons.

"Now then, what shall we write?"

Her glee was evident, but Timothy was none the wiser. "Write?"

Her head bobbed, and Timothy tried to focus on her

words rather than the way that her hair was almost unpinned around her left ear, the chestnut waves moving dangerously.

"Write. Write messages. Is that not what you said – leaving little treasures behind?"

His laugh was almost unbelieving. "Treasures – messages – write them down! You cannot be serious." And yet he desperately hoped that she was. Sent to Weymouth for her health? Cordelia was a woman that you could not cure, because there was nothing wrong with her.

Her smile was broad, and her matching laughter quieter than his own. "Well, why not? Let us give the people of Weymouth something to gossip about."

Cordelia leaned over, shawl once again readjusted, and began to write. He knew that he should not, knew that it was against all sense of propriety and gentility, but at his central core he was a man, and a man who could appreciate the female form. The way that she leaned, the careful way that she bit her lip as she considered what to write – it was enough to get any man's blood heated, and his was almost boiling.

"There; do you approve?"

Startled from his reverie, he took in the five pieces of paper that she had thrust to his face. They read:

The man who truly loves you needs a sign – give him one

They know. Run.

What would your mother say?

The King's next visit to Weymouth will occur on a Tuesday.

Money without happiness is like honey without bread; it gets everywhere, but you cannot enjoy it.

A grin wider than one he thought he could ever experience spread over Timothy's face. "Where did you read these from?"

Cordelia looked at him oddly, her eyebrows scrunched together. "Read them? I did not read them from anywhere,

I plucked them out of my mind. Do you like them?"

"Like them? They are gold!"

It took less than a minute for them to secrete the five notes into different books around the circulating library, and then they quietly left without speaking to the attendant again.

"But you did not get the book by William Gifford," Cordelia said after they had reached the seashore once again, and were walking along it.

She had taken off both shoes again, walking in the sand barefoot, and Timothy stepped in her footprints. "It will not be going anywhere fast, I would think – he is not a particularly desired author. I will get my turn. I am a patient man."

"Too patient, if you ask me! What about this woman you have spent the last three days waiting for?" A curl of hair escaped and she tucked it absentmindedly behind her ear. "Do you not think that your patience should run out eventually?"

He shrugged. The wind was tugging at her shawl and he was glad that he had not brought his top hat with him that day. "Eventually. But I have been corresponding with her for – why, many months now. She is an elderly friend of the family, and I feel honour bound to meet with her."

Cordelia stooped down to pick up a piece of seaweed yet again, and began twisting it around and around her fingers. Timothy now had the almost impossible task of concentrating on where he was placing his feet – riding boots poorly designed for sand striding – and not becoming absorbed in following the progress of those slender digits.

"She is an incredible writer, actually," he said, hoping that continued conversation would distract him from one problem and keep his mind on another. "I cannot help but find her fascinating, and her turn of phrase is most captivating. I happily anticipate each letter that I receive, and am frequently disappointed at their brevity."

She laughed as her shawl was almost blown away from her completely, and then said, "You must be disappointed, then, to miss her."

"I am," was his reply, but it was not altogether a truthful one. For, he told himself, if Miss Honeyfield and her striking golden heart-shaped locket had arrived this morning, he would be spending the hours speaking to an elderly and rather unwell (by the sounds of it) lady. This time with Cordelia would be lost to him, and he was finding that any time not spent with her was time wasted.

"Look!" She pointed to an area of Weymouth far from them where small shapes were being gently lowered into the sea by ponies. "Are those the bathing machines?"

"They are indeed," Timothy replied, his gaze more occupied with Cordelia herself than her topic of interest. "Have you seen one before?"

She shook her head, more hair flying out into the wind. "No, but . . . I have always wanted to go swimming in the sea. I have been told that there is absolutely nothing like it in the world, and I do not consider my life complete without that experience."

"You would be hard pressed to do it now, in March!" He stared out at the freezing waters, and shuddered. The wind was cold enough. "But if you stayed long enough in Weymouth for the season to truly begin, you could try sea bathing."

Cordelia was still dancing out ahead of him. "Do you not think swimming itself a beneficial idea then?"

Timothy shrugged. "Many people choose to be dipped."

She stared. "Dipped?"

"They go down in one of the bathing machines, and then are gently lowered by someone into the water. Usually they cannot swim, so they just float there. Of course, dippers are much more easy to regulate – it is the swimmers who need to follow the restrictions."

"Restrictions?"

"Bathing restrictions." His boots were still struggling across the sand, but she seemed to be dancing on air. "They segregate male and female swimmers, you see, and there is a stretch of rope over there," and he pointed, "where the line is."

"So, men and women cannot swim together?"

He shook his head with a smile. "That would be quite scandalous! No, in season there is usually a gentleman there to ensure that people swim on the correct side of the line. There is much the same rule in many of the sea bathing towns along the coast: Brighton I think, and Ramsgate also."

She laughed, and twirled around, shawl fluttering in the breeze. "Is it not marvellous and ridiculous that even something as wild as the sea has to be tamed by our petty human ideals of decorum, and polite society?"

He laughed gently. "Your obsession and love of the ocean conquers all things, does it not?"

Cordelia raised an eyebrow mischievously. "Do you think I was a mermaid in another life?"

Before he could answer, her shawl, battered by the wind, flew off one shoulder and Cordelia caught at it with a laugh, dancing forward and running into the wind. Timothy smiled, and his pulse raced. This woman, there was no one at all to compare to her. It would be impossible to be bored in her presence, and there would never be a minute that you could truly predict.

What was this feeling? He examined it as he watched her wrestle with her shawl once more, eventually losing the fight as it went cascading off into the breeze, caught finally, and coming down right at the water's edge.

As he hurried to retrieve the shawl, his hands became cold and wet as he lifted the shawl from the tide line. Was this . . . love?

"Thank you!" Cordelia was out of breath and she beamed at him as she held out her hand for her shawl. "It is sopping wet I suppose, but it cannot be helped."

Timothy stared at her.

"Do not worry about carrying it though, I am quite happy to wear it slightly damp," she continued, hand still outstretched. When he said nothing, silent and still as a statue, she repeated, "thank you."

But he did not move. He could not tear his eyes away from the large golden heart-shaped locket that was hanging around her neck.

Obscured by the shawl. That is the only way that he could have missed it, have not seen it each of the three days he had met her. Surely, he could not be so blind as to have seen it and not put the pieces together? Miss C Honeyfield. Cordelia. Two women come to Weymouth for their health, two women meeting a doctor, two women meeting at the same point every day. But not two women. One woman.

Miss Cordelia Honeyfield. How could he have been so blind? What were the chances that another person would have chosen the exact time and location for meeting? And why on earth did he not ask for her full name – why did he not give his?

"You look rather exhausted." Her words were faint and far off, and Timothy concentrated. They were still standing by the shore line, the incoming tide now washing over his boots and her feet. The seaweed was still in her hand, and the shawl in his. "Time to get back to dry land, if you ask me."

Timothy opened his mouth, and then closed it again. This was the time to say something, to reveal the mistake, to disabuse her of the assumption that they did not know each other. Now. Do it now.

"I am tired," he said quietly. "Let us head back to the shore."

CHAPTER FOUR

"And you're telling me that she has absolutely no idea who you are?"

The voice sounded incredulous, and Timothy winced as his friend's words carried across the crowd. He did not need the entire Assembly Rooms to start asking awkward questions of him; he had enough of that from his own conscience.

"Do not be a fool," he replied curtly. "She knows that I am Timothy."

John's eyes widened and his mouth fell open. "And you honestly think that that's enough to prevent her from finding out the truth and railing you about it for all eternity?"

Timothy shrugged, but his nonchalance was forced. "Perhaps that would not be the end of the world . . . if she stayed around to crow at me, at least I would still be with her . . ."

His companion shook his head in disbelief, and took a glass of punch from a passing waiter. "Well I think you're mad," he said flatly. "Mad."

Timothy watched his friend drink thirstily, and sighed. Was he mad? It had been mere hours since he had uncovered Miss Cordelia Honeyfield's identity, and he had been wracked with guilt ever since. Not even tonight's invitation to the Assembly Rooms, the lively music performed with such gaiety, nor the delightful food that had been laid on by the Royal Hotel, had been enough to lift his spirits.

"Besides," John continued, a smile spreading over his face as he beheld the room before him, "are there not sufficient young ladies in Weymouth for you without mooning over one in particular? You're the youngest doctor for miles around – I could never understand how you finished your studies so quickly – do you not think that any other woman could interest you?"

John's gaze roved over the coiffed hair in the French style, silk dresses with their corsets tightened to within an inch of their wearers' life, and the wafting of a dozen perfumes in the air.

Mere hours ago, Timothy had been laughing with Cordelia, wandering around Weymouth with her, leaving the strangest notes in books for unsuspecting readers to discover. His smile was unbidden, unconscious. All of these pretty puffed up ladies who were promenading before them – it may satisfy John, but he had had a taste of something real, something that satisfied. Something that he wanted.

"That's a new one." John's words interrupted his meditation, and he jerked his head to glance where his friend was pointing – and his mouth fell open.

Cordelia had just walked through the large doors into the Assembly Rooms, and she was miserable. Timothy could tell why almost immediately; instead of the looser, more flowing style of gown that he had seen her in previously, she had been trussed up in a Marie Antoinette style gown with ribbons beyond ribbons cascading down the back. Her hair had been powdered, and if he was not mistaken, she was wearing court shoes.

"My my, not a bird happy in its cage," murmured John.

Timothy swallowed. Surely here, in this alcove on the other side of the room, with the musicians a much more attractive sight to their left, they would remain unseen. They could have been spotted, for she was looking across the room vaguely as if to find an acquaintance, any acquaintance – but then a hand grasped her wrist, and Mrs Chambers led her over to the other side of the room where the Master of Ceremonies was standing.

John tutted under his breath. "I must say, the French court may lead our fashions now in the 1790s, but I do wish those poor girls would loosen their corsets – you know my sister told me of a lady who actually fainted in Almack's last week. Couldn't revive her until they cut the cords, and of course it was a true-blue scandal because the man whose pocket knife they borrowed –"

"That is her, John." Timothy had stopped listening to his friend, and his gaze was still fixed on her. "That is Cordelia."

"Cordelia?" John blinked, uncomprehending, and then he sighed with understanding. "Oh, Cordelia. Which one?"

Timothy could feel his heart pounding, and if he was not mistaken there was a bead of sweat soaking into his cravat.

"Walsingham!"

He started, and looked confused at John who was shaking his head. "I've never seen you act like this over a woman before, Timothy. She is the woman that you have been writing to – the elderly woman, who has come here for the sea air? What has got into you?"

Timothy was not sure. He had attended his fair share of Assemblies, both here in Weymouth and in London; had seen many a pretty face dance before him tantalisingly; but none had moved him so much as to affect him. Cordelia was different; even the temperature in the room seemed to change when she stepped into it, and the air around him seemed more solid, more difficult to breathe in, more like quicksand dragging him down into a warm abyss.

"You're quite done for, you know." John's voice jerked him back to the conversation. The music had stopped. Those couples who had been entertaining the standing crowds – and indulging in the one chance to speak in undertones to their partners – now applauded the musicians, and retired to the edges of the room, a murmuring chatter increasing in volume as comparisons of technique were made, comments on general suitability aired, and mothers clucked around their eligible daughters.

Cordelia, a relative outsider to the company, stood to one side. He could see that Mrs Chambers, whilst keeping a close eye on her charge, was not strapped to her side. She was now talking to a gentleman of the town, her back turned to Cordelia who stood silently, looking around the room as though searching for a friendly shore.

Timothy bit his lip. "I should have told her yesterday," he said in a low tone to his friend, turning towards him to keep his voice low. "As soon as I saw that locket, I should have realised that was the opportunity to be open – and now the situation is completely hopeless."

"Hopeful, I'd say," John replied matter-of-factly. "I mean, what have you done wrong? Made an honest mistake about a young lady, which you can now rectify. After all, isn't this your perfect opportunity?"

Shaking his head, he replied, "I do not think that there is ever going to be a perfect opportunity – no, listen, John," said Timothy, preventing his friend's interruption, "you have not heard her talk about this doctor who has sent her here. She did not know – does not know, rather, that I was he, and she has been decidedly uncompromising on her opinions of him."

The lead violinist was tapping on his music stand, calling one of the other musicians back to the group. Timothy watched as the wandering artiste began to drink liberally from the punch bowl. He tried not to laugh, then caught the sound of an uncontrolled snort from the other side of the room.

He grinned. He would know her laugh anywhere, even after just three days' familiarity.

John was speaking, and Timothy tried to attend to his words. "Surely she can't hold such an innocent mistake against you."

"Who says it is innocent?"

John blinked. "Well, you do!"

"But that is my point," Timothy tried to explain. "'Tis only my word against hers, and no one would believe me over an innocent young woman!"

"Timothy Walsingham, my friend, you get ahead of yourself." John placed a calming hand on his arm, and smiled reassuringly. "There is no talk yet of proving yourself, or defending your honour, or anything like that. Just think instead of the simple facts."

But how could he think of the simple facts, when all he wanted to do was stride across the room and take Cordelia in his arms and – no, he must not think that, she did not even know who he was yet!

"The facts are," John was continuing, "that you prefer a young woman who seems to prefer you, and there is a little confusion about identities. That is all. For all you know, a simple introduction from the Master of Ceremonies, goodness gracious me what are the chances, aha, isn't this an excellent story that we can tell our grandchildren. Problem solved."

Wild mirth was pouring from his friend, but Timothy did not think it was funny. "I concede that it could be solved . . . and yet it could become a tangle from which I never escape."

The two friends watched as the Master of Ceremonies worked his way around the room, smiling at all, nodding at some, clasping the hands of others.

Timothy sighed. All he wanted was to be out of the damned tight waistcoat and be home, where he could think. "I do not want to become tainted by her idea of this doctor."

"You are the doctor." John helpfully reminded him.

Timothy glowered. "Thank you."

Ignoring his friend's chuckles, Timothy reached for a glass of wine as it was paraded past him. The Master of Ceremonies was talking to Cordelia, although Mrs Chambers appeared to be doing most of the talking.

And then the unthinkable happened. Cordelia looked up, and their eyes met.

Hers bright and sparkling, his deep and grey; sparks of desire and confusion travelled down both bodies as they were drawn together by an unfathomable tide.

"You do not think . . . " breathed Timothy.

John laughed. "I do believe that the Master of Ceremonies is bringing your Cordelia right over here. Goodness, Timothy, who would have credited it!"

He was not sure whether his heart had stopped beating, or whether it was going so fast that it was almost a blur. This could not be happening; surely fate would not draw him such a hand as this? But there she was, gliding like a ship across the waves, and his feet were glued to the floor as though they were anchored there.

Move. Move now.

"Good evening, sir." John's voice called out, a lighthouse in the room, guiding Timothy back to shore. "Tis quite an honour for us to converse with the Master of Ceremonies."

Mr Archibald, a pompous man who enjoyed nothing better than to be admired, smiled broadly. "Ah, Mr Stanford, you know that the pleasure is all mine."

The two men exchanged pleasantries and Timothy stared at Cordelia. She stared back, a cheeky smile on her face but her hands demurely clasped together at the front of her gown. He tried to ignore the stirrings growing deeper than he had ever imagined possible, and attempted to focus on the conversation.

". . . new to Weymouth, I took it upon myself to

introduce her to some of the respectable gentlemen of the town," Mr Archibald was saying.

Timothy tried not to show the alarm he was feeling, but his feet unconsciously shuffled and his neck twitched. Was this not the exact nightmare that he had hoped to avoid?

Cordelia curtsied, deep and low, and Timothy tried not to gaze too much at the subtle curves that suddenly became much more visible. The heart locket was still there.

"May I introduce Mr Stanford?"

John bowed at the Master of Ceremonies' words, and now Timothy's heart was beating so fast his ribcage may explode. The musicians were tuning for their next piece but they sounded a long way off, and he was starting to be able to see his heartbeat as his pulse raced across his eyes –

Mr Archibald was now gesturing to him. This was it. This was the instant that he lost her.

"And this –"

"Oh, I know who this is." Cordelia's voice was clear as she interrupted the Master of Ceremonies. "This man and I are known to each other."

Timothy blinked. Then a broad smile grew on his face. "Indeed. Would you grace me with the next dance?"

Cordelia felt, rather than spoke the answer. She had not even admitted to herself that she had hoped that the tall man she was starting to admire more than any other man, would ask her to dance, and now here he was, doing just that.

She nodded. His arm was offered, and she took it without checking with Mrs Chambers – who in any case, had already found another woman to converse with, and seemed perfectly happy to allow Cordelia to stride off with this gentleman.

The wool of Timothy's frockcoat was coarse under Cordelia's fingertips. Her gloves had been abandoned at a table several minutes before, and she was glad now; every touch was more special, more intimate when it was made without the interference of gloves.

"You look . . ." Timothy was speaking at such a whisper as they made their way to the middle of the room that she could barely hear him, and she lifted her head to him, noting the smile and the seriousness on his face. "You look beautiful, Cordelia."

Try as she might to prevent it, a blush washed over her face and the tingling in her stomach, the one that she had tried to ignore as soon as she saw him when she had entered the room, returned.

"Thank you," was all she could murmur in return before they parted to face each other.

There were seven other couples in this set, and the musicians seemed impatient to start, beginning so quickly that one young lady had to push her partner into position. Laughter rang out through the room, and Cordelia giggled, dispelling the uncomfortable nerves that had suddenly flowed through her. Why should she be nervous? She knew Timothy well enough for a country dance. Why, they had discussed William Gifford together.

And then something happened that she did not expect. The first melody of the music struck up, and she stepped towards Timothy, and his blazing gaze took her off guard. Before she could regain her composure, their hands were lifting and they touched, and she could not help but gasp at the intensity of it: skin to skin, flesh to flesh, neither of them wearing gloves. It was as though she had been burned.

There was ringing in her ears that had nothing to do with the music, and he stumbled as he made his way back to his set. Did he feel it too?

They came together again, and this time, he spoke. "Cordelia, there is something – something about you that I cannot understand, and I want to."

Her heart fluttered again. "I –"

The cruel dance drew them away from each other again; all they could do was look; but the force in his eyes almost made her take a step backwards. Emotions stirred in her that were something akin to . . . love?

"I had hoped you would be here," she managed to breathe the next time they came close, but all else she had planned to say was lost when he placed his hand around her waist. The dance demanded it, and Cordelia accepted it willingly, the heat of his hand piercing not her gown but her very soul. This man – this man could touch her anywhere and she would let him, she would want him to, she would –

They broke apart again, and Cordelia swallowed as she twirled around the woman who stood on her left. What on earth was she thinking, what was she doing? Blushing furiously now, she tried to focus on the dance and not the handsome man who was mirroring her every move.

But she could not stay away from him. Even if the dance had not ordained their paths to meet again, she would have sought him out willingly.

"Timothy," her voice low as they clasped hands once more, not taking her eyes from his, "I do not think that there is a man in the world who I would rather be with, right now, than you."

"And I do not think that I would let you."

They parted, and Cordelia stared at him. Did he say . . . this was intolerable, she must speak to him properly without all of this stepping away and stepping forward. Did he mean . . . ?

The dance was coming to a close now, and Cordelia hated the musicians for speeding through their bars so quickly, a tide eager to kiss the shore. Could they not see that every moment spent here with Timothy was one she would treasure?

For the last time, they came together, her arms leaning back as he encircled her waist with his hands. But instead of following decorum and leaning backwards to mirror her, he leaned forward. Cordelia could feel his warm breath on her neck, and the impulse to lean forwards and meet his lips with hers overwhelmed her.

"Cordelia," said his voice, low so that no one else could hear but her, "Cordelia, I think I –"

Applause drowned out his last words. The musicians had stopped, but Timothy had not let her go. Cordelia's chest fluttered up and down, out of control. Slowly, she raised her neck. His face was mere inches from hers; all she had to do was move her lips and they would kiss. She wanted to, but she waited, hesitant.

He swallowed, and she was captivated by the movement of his neck. He was undoubtedly male, this close, and she could feel the strength in his arms as he held her tight.

"Cordelia," he repeated, and now his voice was jagged with barely repressed emotion. "Cordelia –"

"Cordelia!" A different voice now called out her name, and suddenly the tight clasp she was nestled in disappeared. Timothy strode away as Mrs Chambers came bustling towards her. "Cordelia, that was an elegant dance. Have you met Mr Yattersly? He is a gentleman of Lyme, Lyme Regis you know, and has come here for . . ."

An hour later in her own room at the Golden Lion, Cordelia stared out of the window at the crescent moon that was reflected like a broken mirror on the ever-shifting waves. Tonight could not have been more perfect if she had planned it herself – perhaps even then. If she closed her eyes, she could still feel the touch of Timothy across her waist, feel his warmth, taste that tantalising promise of a kiss that never came.

But it was wrong to think of a man so, surely it was? She was not here to matchmake, she was here to . . . well, return to full health, according to her father. What was she here for, if not for an adventure?

The memory of his laughter made her smile in turn, standing alone in her room. He was unlike any man she had ever met; gentle, and intelligent, and strangely happy for her to do almost anything she wanted. Attractive characteristics, certainly, but he was something more. There was a depth to him, more mysterious than the deeps of the ocean where no one knew what lived there. There was much more to Timothy than met the eye.

Her eye fell upon the paper and ink pot on the desk, beside her bed. Her face fell. Dances and beachside strolls aside, there was one thing still to be done.

Seating herself at the desk, fighting the tiredness that was creeping over her with every stolen minute, Cordelia began to write.

Friday 12th – or Saturday 13th March, 1790. Weymouth
Dr Walsingham,

What a disappointment you are turning out to be. I waited for you as long as I could, you know, but when there is better company to be had, I must go where delight and diversion take me. Of course, there is not much of a contest when you decide that seeing me is simply not inviting enough to bother to attend our appointment, but you will be glad to hear that I found quite enough amusement to entertain me throughout the day. I do, however, have the promise to my father to keep, and I feel that it is only right that you sort out your own affairs when I have been most obliging.

Perhaps it is the location that does not suit? I hate to think that it could be the company, and so I propose a different meeting place altogether. It seems that the promenade is a little difficult for you, and I suppose that one wishing to avoid crowds would find it most arduous. I have it on excellent authority – local, mind you, and dependable as the ocean – that the bathing restrictions are rarely used, and where the line is often drawn could be a simple place to meet. It is directly opposite the bathing machines, where the beach becomes segregated. Let us say, tomorrow at midday? That should give you enough time to find an excuse not to come.

I am becoming impatient to meet you, Dr Walsingham, and if you insist on hiding yourself away I shall have to come and hunt you out. Let us both pray, for your sake, that it does not come to that.

Until then I shall remain,

Miss C Honeyfield

CHAPTER FIVE

The last of the bathing machines was hitched up to its obliging pony, and it began its slow and steady descent to the water's edge. The man who stood by the pony's head was evidently calming it down, and Cordelia could see why. She would not want to walk backwards down a slope with such heavy cargo attached to her shoulders.

But that was the way these bathing machines worked, of course. In mere seconds, the swimmers would be able to explore the ocean freely without the inappropriate gazes of strollers along the beach, and they could take in all the goodness that the salty spray offered. It seemed to be beckoning many people into its delightful waters, and somewhere deep inside herself, Cordelia found herself drawn to the blue swirls of the ocean. What must it be like to swim in the sea?

Footsteps sounded behind her; heavy, made by a man in large boots. She did not turn her head, fascinated by the meandering path that the waves took across the shoreline.

"Cordelia?"

Startled, a voice that she recognised had just spoken her name. Timothy was standing before her, his top hat tucked underneath his arm.

"What on earth . . ." She stared at him, amazed. "What are the chances that you would come here this afternoon, too!"

A rush of pleasure, unexplained and unquestioned, rushed over her, and she became uncomfortably conscious of what she was wearing. To think that it was only a mere twelve hours since they had last seen each other, touched each other, danced in the candlelight as though no one else was there . . .

For a wild moment, Cordelia saw visions in her head of him dropping down to one knee and declaring his love for her – for a wild moment, she imagined accepting him. It was a wild thought indeed, to live here with a man that made her feel so alive, in Weymouth, the beach she was growing to love so well.

And then she saw the way that he swallowed, and stared down at the ground.

"What are the chances?" She murmured to herself. It was not as though Weymouth was a particularly large place, after all, and this area was more secluded than the others, with few places to be spotted. It was not possible to see her from the street.

Timothy swallowed again, and Cordelia rose from her seat slowly. Suspicion, only a seedling at first, was starting to grow. She had made his acquaintance four days ago – four short days, a period that was nothing. There were glove makers with whom she had spent more time, and she did not even know whether they had wives, or children, or where they lived.

The wind blew between them, and Cordelia's long skirts fluttered, causing her to step into it to prevent being pushed over. The sand shifted with her, and she almost lost her balance.

What was it she knew about him, really? It had not even struck her mind, to ask his full name; he was just Timothy to her, a man who could have come from anywhere. Perhaps he had followed her here this morning;

perhaps he had been watching her for days.

"I do not understand," she said uncertainly. "Why –"

"Coincidence is a strange thing, is it not?" He interrupted her and his smiling face seemed to plead with her to not ask too many questions. "It was a coincidence that first led to our meeting, do you remember?"

"Remember? It was four days ago!" Cordelia tried to keep calm, but there was a quaver in her tone that she could not completely hide. Why had she come here to meet Dr Walsingham without Mrs Chambers? She had insisted that her chaperone stay resting this morning after the extravagances of last night, and now she regretted her confidence in coming here alone. "Why is it that the only person whom I have spoken to in the whole of Weymouth is you, Timothy, and you seem to be popping up wherever I go?"

He swallowed again. "Weymouth is a small place, Cordelia, much smaller than London. You will have to accustom yourself to seeing the same people over and –"

"But I am not seeing the same people," she said, "I am seeing you. I have – I have seen you a lot, and I am not even sure that I know why."

Timothy walked towards her with a smile, and stopped inches from her. "I have enjoyed our time together; have you not?"

He scrutinised her face, hoping beyond hope to see some excitement there in seeing him, but all he could see was concern, and fear. He was stupid, stupid not to see this coming. Of course she was starting to question things. He could not blame her, and if he could only be brave enough to say something . . .

"I think I will go to go back to my lodgings." Her words were resolute, and she picked up the book that she had laid beside her in the sand. The swiftness of her movement scattered more grains into its pages, but she ignored it. Haste was her primary concern.

It was the exact opposite of what he wanted, and

Timothy's heart sank. "No, Cordelia, please stay."

"No, I would rather go," she spoke decidedly, and she moved past him quickly, her shawl resting on her elbows as it slipped down from her shoulders.

"Please wait." It was a movement more instinctive than considered, and it was done in an instant. His hand reached out and grabbed at her arm. He surprised himself with his own strength, and Cordelia swayed, unable to move forward as her arm was held in that vice-like grip.

She could not help her eyes darting over to him, and he could see that there was real panic in them now. They were moving around her, taking in the deserted area, with no one else in sight, let alone hearing distance.

"Let me go," were her words, and there was fear in them now as her eyes widened at the solid grip that he had on her arm.

He could not think, his blood was roaring through his ears like a tidal wave as he spoke. "Miss Honeyfield, let me explain —"

Stillness.

Cordelia had stopped struggling against him. He had dropped his grip. The two of them stood, mere inches apart, in complete silence.

It was a squawking argument between two seagulls feet behind her that brought them back to life.

"How do you know my name?"

The whisper was low, but clear enough for Timothy to catch it, and it tore at his heart. Why had he not said something yesterday? He berated himself. All this would have been avoided, and now you have lost any hope of trust.

"How do you know it?" Cordelia repeated, stronger now. "Because I do not recall ever giving you my full name, and there are few here who know it. How did you know that I was going to be here? Who are you?"

He almost choked, as though he had swallowed his own tongue, and then he realised that it was a sinking feeling as his heart plummeted. There was nothing for it now; she was going to find out.

He took out of the left pocket of his greatcoat a letter, written on dark cream paper.

Cordelia stared at the paper that she saw every day, and snatched it from his hand before Timothy could say another word. Striding away from him, she could hear him call after her, "Wait, Cordelia – let me explain!"

"This is my paper," she muttered to herself, and pulling out its contents, "and this is my letter." Her eyes scanned over the lines that had not existed until she had put pen to paper less than twenty-four hours ago: It seems that the promenade is a little difficult for you . . . I have it on excellent authority – local, mind you, and dependable as the ocean – that the bathing restrictions are rarely used . . . I am becoming impatient to meet you, Dr Walsingham, and if you insist on hiding yourself away I shall have to come and hunt you out . . .

She raised her eyes from the ink, and turned slowly. Timothy was staring at her, a wretched expression across his face.

"Dr Walsingham."

She had meant it as a statement, and it came out as a whisper. He nodded.

Embarrassment shot through her like an arrow, and although she did not bleed, the heat of her shame poured from her chest to the rest of her body.

"You must have been laughing at me all week," she said thickly, voice full of emotion, "walking around Weymouth with me, talking to me as though I were a stranger, when in truth the whole time –"

"No!" Timothy interjected heartily. "No, it was not like that!"

Cordelia laughed drily. "Really? You consider this springtide meeting to be natural? Because I find it incredibly hard to believe that you did not think me a complete fool when I spoke of my idiot doctor conniving with my darling Papa to send me away and 'be cured'!"

The arguing seagulls had settled their dispute and soared off into the air, but there seemed to be no easy way out of this conversation. Timothy stared at the beautiful and outraged woman before him, and the heat of shame that had been flowing through him turned to something else – something that he should certainly not be feeling about a woman who was so angry with him. How had he not seen it before? When he put this woman, a woman unlike any other, together with the intelligent and entertaining woman in the letters . . . surely this was the perfect mixture of salty breeze and sweet sunshine?

"Cordelia, I was never laughing at you." His words, meant to be reassuring, fell flat.

She was shaking her head, and the smile on her face had gone. Now there was hurt and confusion. "I cannot believe that you did not tell me that it was you – that you were Dr Walsingham."

"I only realised who you were yesterday afternoon!" Timothy tried to defend himself, but every word that he uttered seemed hollow. Would he have believed himself? His awkwardness was doing him no favours, and he needed to convince her. "It was your locket; I had not seen it before yesterday, when you dropped your shawl, remember? And that was when I realised – but I did not know how to say, in that instant, who I was, and then last night –"

"I am sure you would have found the words, if you had wanted to!" Cordelia spoke harshly, and there was no warmth in her eyes. Book clasped to her chest shielding her, the heart-shaped locket peeked out between it and her graceful neck, and her lips moved before he reminded himself to pay attention to what she was saying. ". . . as a spy for my father. It was not enough, evidently, that I was sent away from home –

"Sent away from home – Cordelia, you have told me yourself that you wanted to come to the seaside!"

"– no, I needed more than a chaperone for him to be completely satisfied, and so here you are to ensure that I do not embarrass myself even further!"

"It was not like that – it is not like that!" Patience finally gone, Timothy strode forward and reached out, placing his hands on her arms. "Damnit, Cordelia, I am a doctor not a jailor! As soon as I met you, I knew that you were not here to be cured, you were here to be put out of the way – but I was enjoying your company far too much to ask why, and the fact that I never placed elderly Miss Honeyfield and the beautiful Cordelia together – can you blame me for not wanting to ruin everything? Does this conversation not give you enough clues as to why I may wish to avoid it?"

She staggered out of reach as though he had burned her with his touch.

"Cordelia," and it was hard to ignore the pleading tones in his own voice now. "Please Cordelia – I think . . . I know that I am falling in love with you, and –"

"Love?" Although the word made her heart quicken, she forced down her emotions. "I do not know you, sir, and I have no wish to. What you do with the rest of your time in Weymouth is up to you. I think I have had enough sea air to last me a lifetime."

No further words were said before she rushed away, sand scattered to the wind behind her as she ran. Timothy stood watching the lone figure disappear into the haze of the sand.

CHAPTER SIX

The smell of salt and fish was almost overwhelming, but Timothy did not let the crowds around the early Monday market prevent him from striding towards his destination.

Cordelia's lodgings. Cordelia Honeyfield, the woman he had known, or thought he had known, or was getting to know, and just as he realised that the elderly woman writing letters and the beautiful young woman always two strides ahead of him dancing in the wind were one and the same person –

"Watch out there!"

He ducked, top hat toppling onto the sand-strewn cobbles as a man with freshly baked bread strode past, his cursory warning shouted too late to prevent the accident.

Timothy continued walking, leaving the hat to sit where it fell. A letter, scrunched and well-read, was grasped in his left hand. An entirely fruitless day he had spent searching throughout Weymouth for her, despite his vague remembrance that she had mentioned her lodgings, and then the answer had been in one of her letters from two weeks ago, all along: I will be staying at the Golden Lion, a place with little glamour for those of little fortune, so it will be the perfect backdrop for me.

And there it was. He had walked past it twice yesterday and had never thought to enquire there, so quiet was it that he could not picture the vibrant, determined Cordelia there. But for Miss Honeyfield? It was an oasis of calm.

The opposite of an oasis of calm met him as soon as he had crossed the threshold and entered a small parlour.

"And what exactly is it that you want here, Dr Walsingham?" The arched tones of Mrs Chambers matched her face, suspicion and mistrust in every syllable.

Timothy swallowed. He was facing a dragon. "Mrs Chambers, how delightful to – "

"I am not sure what you said to her," she cut in, folding the gloves in her hands as she spoke, eyes never leaving him, "but she is not happy with you, I can tell you that for nothing."

"And she is within her right to be – that is," he said hastily as Mrs Chambers' mouth opened angrily, "I have done no harm to her, of course, but there has been a confusion."

"Hmmmph."

That seemed to be the only reply that he was likely to get from her, but he waited for a minute to see whether she would say any more. When the silence had lingered on longer than he would have preferred, Timothy tried again. His cravat was choking him, and he wanted to be back on the beach, surrounded by the comfort of the wild wind.

"I merely want to explain, Mrs Chambers, that is all – I have no wish to press upon her, or anything . . . well, of that sort." Timothy hoped that she could not tell he was lying. He desperately wanted to press Cordelia to listen to him, to give him the chance to explain, to understand that –

"I cannot understand why there is such a fuss, me." Now the last of the gloves were folded, the basket was placed on her hip as she glared astutely at him. "Soon as I saw you, I recognised you. There is nothing better than a precise description for knowing a person, and the

Reverend had been most particular that I would know you on sight. He was concerned, his sister being sent so far away, and without family beside her. And so I did. Why do you think I let you continue on with Miss Honeyfield?"

He blinked. "You . . . you knew who I was?"

Mrs Chambers snorted. "What sort of chaperone do you take me for? You think I would let her wander through Weymouth – Weymouth! – with a gentleman with no name, rank, fortune? You think she is here to be married off to anyone who would take an interest, the first man to bother speaking to her?"

"But, but," he spluttered, "but you never told her who I was."

His words prompted a response that he had not expected. Before he could escape her, Mrs Chambers was standing before him, her brow furrowed and anger in her eyes. "I am not here to make formal introductions," she hissed. "'Tis my fault, I suppose, that you did not think to give her your full name? It is down to me, is it, to ensure that full family histories are given before any meetings?"

Startled and slightly alarmed at the angry woman, Timothy took a step backwards, and his shoulders slumped. "No. No of course not, Mrs Chambers. This misunderstanding is of my own doing, and mine alone to untangle."

He turned, and walked towards the door.

"And hers."

The two words made him pause, and checking over his shoulder he saw that a wry smile was now across Mrs Chambers' face.

"She did not tell you her full name either, did she?" And now the smile widened. "Sounds to me, you are both victims of your own nonsense, if you ask me. Now, why do you not go down to the beach, opposite the circulating library? I think you will find someone there who is rather eager to speak to you."

Dr Timothy Walsingham finally found Miss Cordelia

Honeyfield walking along the beach, skirts up to her knees, feet paddling in the sea.

It was Cordelia; even from half a mile off, he could tell. There was only one person who danced in that way, with spray kicked up at regular intervals.

Hurried feet picked up the pace as he rushed forwards ever faster. It was astonishing that no one had spoken to her for keeping her long billowing skirts that high, almost a sail in the wind that was gusting around her.

And then Timothy stopped dead, about twenty feet from her. A fiery lurch tugged at his stomach as he watched her. There was no one like her, and he could not ignore the undeniably physical response that he had to watching her just . . . be. Why be like everyone else when you could be yourself?

Suddenly, she appeared aware that she was being watched, and she turned her head about her, searching for the lingering eyes – and theirs met.

"There is no need to panic," Cordelia called out, her smile not faltering but the warmth behind it dying. "And there is no need to report to my darling Papa."

Timothy took a step forward, and then another one. He said nothing.

"I have not gone mad, you know," Cordelia continued, kicking at a wave as it rolled onto the golden shores. Now that he was closer, he could see that her mother's heart-shaped locket was bouncing from her chest as each large kick hit the spray. "All I wanted was to feel the sea between my toes before I go back to the smog and soot of London. No sea bathing for me, naturally, cannot have reports of my misbehaviour fed back to my father!"

There was no response from him, except the continuation of his walk. She stared at him, and unconsciously took a step back, walking deeper into the ocean. Her skirts, already heavy with sand, dried salt, and water, dropped. They moved around her legs in the water, gently following the tide. None of this slowed down his walk, and Cordelia took another step backwards, the water now bobbing a few inches below her knees.

He was now a few steps away from her, and her voice did wobble as she said, "I have discharged myself from your medical care, so you do not have to concern yourself with me any further, you know."

Timothy stood before her. There were only three or four inches between them now, and her breathing was causing her chest to rise and fall in a jagged motion. His eyes, as grey as the sea was that day, never left her face, and she found herself unable to stand the fierce gaze.

Her eyes fell, and she swallowed. "You are all wet."

"Yes," said Timothy simply. And then he reached out, drew her to him, and lowered his desperately searching mouth onto hers.

CHAPTER SEVEN

Pent up passion poured down onto her lips, and Cordelia revelled in the kiss. At once forceful and gentle, Timothy only took from her what she was willing to give – though his desire for her was obvious. He had one hand clasped tightly around her waist, drawing her into his warm and strong chest where her hands were clinging as the waves pushed them backwards and forwards. His other hand was at the base of her neck, fingers entangled in her hair as it shed its pins and started to roll down her back.

She had never felt this way before – nothing else compared to this. Warmth was flooding through her veins turning her at once burning hot and freezing cold, and the tug of the tide on her skirts was nothing to the tugging in her heart that was pulling her towards him. Her heart was fluttering faster than she had ever experienced, and she could not help but let out a solitary moan as he delved deeper into her mouth, his tongue gently caressing hers.

This was what it was to be alive, thought Cordelia wildly, this was living, this was true freedom! And with a man whom she had met less than a week before! Try as she might to find something wrong with this kiss that was leaving her completely breathless, it felt completely right;

as though she had pulled into port.

"Oh, Cordelia," he murmured in her ear as he wrenched his lips from hers. "I cannot tell you – I do not have the words to –"

Her eyelids fluttered open as she took in the wildness in his eyes and matched it by lifting her willing lips up to him once more. He groaned as he sunk into her, the kiss stronger this time, and more certain.

This was a true man, one that made her feel stirrings she had never countenanced for herself. Why, thought Cordelia as her hands wandered past his cravat and into the dark locks of hair, if she took the caring and concerned man in her letters and placed them alongside the strong, entertaining, and kind man before her, she could almost say that she had found the perfect man! Add to the mix this heady yearning that was physically overpowering her . . .

A wave, larger than the others, crashed into them, soaking them on one side and breaking them finally apart. Their laughter was matched by the cries of the seagulls as they soared through the air above them.

Timothy lifted a hand to her cheek, and smiled gently. "Here you are; the woman that I first found in a letter, and then on a beach. Like driftwood looking for a friendly shore, you were deposited before me and I had not even valued it until it had been swept away from me."

"And yet here I am," she whispered, heat still flooding through her body. "I had not drifted far."

"I will dedicate my life to ensuring that you never drift too far away ever again." His voice was determined, and she could not help but beam at it.

"I am still most aggrieved." Her tone was mockingly haughty, but her smile did not disappear. "It was most wrong of you to continue the pretence once you realised who I was."

He nodded. "I know. But I was afraid that I would lose you – that you would think I had known all along, and then you would disappear and I would never have got the chance to really explain how I feel."

She raised an eyebrow. "I hope you are ready to repent completely, for I shall not permit such trickery again."

His answer was a kiss, and it lasted so long that his breath was almost stolen from him, so lost in her he became.

"In that case," Cordelia murmured eventually, "there is only one thing left to do."

He raised an eyebrow. "Just one?"

She nodded, now nestled happily in his arms and unwilling to move. A wicked smile danced across her lips as she said, "Miss Cordelia Honeyfield. Pleased to make your acquaintance."

Timothy laughed. May she never change, this strange woman of his who never ceased to amaze him. He tried to contain his laughter as he replied, "Dr Timothy Walsingham. How would you like to change your name to mine?"

No response was required; no verbal response, anyway. Cordelia's intentions were made perfectly clear as she kissed him hungrily, another wave breaking over them and coating them with a glistening layer of salty water as they clung to each other in the ever-shifting tide.

EPILOGUE

The clatter of the carriage on cobbles grated on him far more than he thought.

"How much longer?" It was more anxiety than irritation that permeated his words, and Cordelia smiled.

"Not much further," she said, placing her hand on his as the carriage rattled to one side. "Though why you are so eager to get there, I do not know."

Timothy looked down at her hand. The golden wedding band that shone on her finger had been there but two weeks, and it still made his heart soar whenever he saw it. Its matching pair was nestled on his own left hand.

"I just want to be out of this carriage," he said restlessly. "I had no idea Weymouth was so far from London – I almost feel seasick in here!"

Cordelia laughed. "Here we are. I said that it would not be far."

He let out a sigh of relief, and then closed his eyes. This journey had been long, that was undeniable, but with every mile they covered, he almost wished that they were back where they started . . .

"He will love you." Her voice broke into his thoughts, and he opened his eyes to see her pulling on her gloves.

"You are a doctor, you are respectable, and you are a wonderful man. He will see that."

"This is the same man that sent you away to be cured of high spirits," muttered Timothy as he opened the door of the carriage and almost stepped onto some horse droppings. "I highly doubt that the welcome will be warm . . ."

He looked around. This was the perfect example of why he lived by the sea; none of this darkness, and grey monotonous skies, and dreary row upon row of houses. Where was the drama in the sky, where was the wind, where was the salt in the air?

Cordelia threw herself out of the carriage and toppled into him. Timothy by now was accustomed to this, and his arms were a willing harbour in which she settled. The feeling of her tightened him, and without giving any thought to their surroundings, his lips found hers and they continued what they had spent the majority of their journey doing.

"Cordelia Honeyfield!"

The astonished cry came from the door before them, and they broke apart hurriedly. Timothy glanced at the man, tall with hair the exact shade of Cordelia's, dressed in clergyman's robes.

"Bertram!"

She left his arms and threw herself towards what must be, Timothy saw now, her brother. There was a similarity in the smile, and it grew beaming on both their faces.

"Cordelia, I had no idea that you were coming home so soon – my letter must not have reached you. She is here!"

She squealed. "No! Oh, Bertram, congratulations! How is Marie? What have you called her?"

Timothy watched as the siblings broke apart, Bertram almost weeping. "We have named her Juliana Cordelia Marie Honeyfield – and you are going to just love her. She is the most perfect child you ever saw."

"I cannot wait to see her!" Cordelia's excitement was

almost overflowing. Timothy could not help but smile; her joy was infectious. Just how long would it take them to notice that he was here?

It turned out to be approximately eleven minutes.

"But Cordelia, we are being so inconsiderate." Bertram finally wrenched himself away from the conversation, and smiled at Timothy. "We have left Dr Walsingham out of our happiness, and the poor man has been waiting patiently to speak to us, I have no doubt. Thank you for bringing my sister home safely, sir."

Nervousness washed through him like the tide roaring in, but Timothy tried not to show it. He stepped forward and bowed. "Reverend Honeyfield, it has been my pleasure to care for your sister these last few weeks."

Bertram held out a hand, and they shook. "Bertram, please," came the only response, but it was accompanied with a smile.

It was now or never.

"Sir, I think it only right," Timothy began, but he was interrupted.

"Is Papa here?" Cordelia asked her brother, a frown of concern appearing briefly across her forehead.

Bertram shook his head. "No, he is at his club – I sent a note informing him of Juliana's arrival yesterday, but he has not yet –"

"We are married."

Timothy blurted it out, and hated himself immediately. There was surely a better way to say it, but how he did not know, and he could bear the suspense no longer. It was said.

At first, Bertram did nothing. Then he looked at his sister, and raised an eyebrow smiling. She nodded, her own face beaming.

Timothy's breath seemed caught in his throat, and the rattle of other carriages behind him on the road seemed to overwhelm his senses.

"Perhaps we should have waited until we had received

your father's permission." He spoke hurriedly, passion in his voice with eyes begging for understanding. "Perhaps it would have been better if we had married here, in London – but we did not want anyone else there, it just seemed so perfect to meet and marry in Weymouth that we –"

"Just got married."

The voice was deep, and gruff, and it came from behind him. Timothy turned. He did not recognise the older gentleman, but he did not need to. The gasp from Cordelia and the groan from Bertram was enough.

Timothy bowed. "Mr Honeyfield."

His father-in-law stared at him, and then his eyes flickered to his daughter. "You love him?"

A hand nestled into Timothy's, and he looked beside him to see the woman he would walk across water for.

"I love him, Papa." Cordelia's voice was strong, and she did not break her father's gaze.

Timothy swallowed, and looked back at Mr Honeyfield – whose gaze had completely shifted, as had his expression. Where there had been dislike and suspicion, there was now joy, a smile breaking across those dark lines.

"Juliana." His eyes glanced over to the couple, and he muttered. "I'll speak with you later."

He strode past them, completely ignoring them, and as Timothy turned to see why, Cordelia gave out a cry of delight.

Standing in the doorway was a woman, tired but content, holding a baby in her arms.

"I think we have been forgotten," Cordelia whispered to him, as they watched the new grandfather beam down at the child. "Perhaps even forgiven."

Timothy nodded. "Perhaps this is the most exciting springtide meeting of them all."

HISTORICAL NOTE

Women's health was treated very differently in the world
of the Regency. Anyone who showed spirit, determination,
and grit, was often labelled as either 'wanton' or 'unwell'.

Cordelia was treated well, comparatively, and I wanted to
ensure that she had a sympathetic doctor to fall in love
with. And who can help it?

Any inaccuracies in this book are, sadly, my own fault, as a
passionate and dedicated author and historian who every
now and again, gets things wrong.

ABOUT THE AUTHOR

Emily Murdoch is a historian and writer. Throughout her career so far she has examined a codex and transcribed medieval sermons at the Bodleian Library in Oxford, designed part of an exhibition for the Yorkshire Museum, worked as a researcher for a BBC documentary presented by Ian Hislop, and worked at Polesden Lacey with the National Trust. She has a degree in History and English, and a Masters in Medieval Studies, both from the University of York. Emily has a medieval series and a Regency novella series published, and is currently working on several new projects.

You can follow her on twitter and instagram @emilyekmurdoch, find her on facebook at www.facebook.com/theemilyekmurdoch, and read her blog at www.emilyekmurdoch.com

Made in the USA
San Bernardino, CA
05 May 2018